The Rex Files

The Baa-Baa Club
Shoo Rayner

Hodder
Children's
Books

First published in Great Britain in 1999
by Hodder Children's Books

ISBN 0 340 71470-0

10   9   8   7   6   5   4   3   2   1

A Catalogue record for this book is available from the British Library

Printed and bound by
The Guernsey Press Co. Ltd, Guernsey, Channel Islands

For
Alice Bleach
(We fell out of a tree together!)

Meet Rex and Franky
on the Internet!
www.shoo-rayner.co.uk

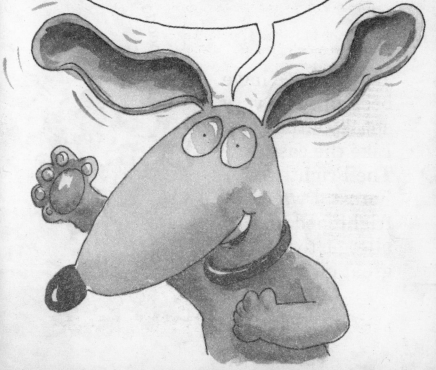

This is my boss, Rex. He's the coolest dog I know. Hardly anything gets past his brilliant, calculating brain.

aaaaaaaaaaachooo!

Together, we have been in some very spooky situations. Like the case of The Frightened Forest. I wasn't frightened, just allergic to the great outdoors!

Rex nearly lost his cool during the case of Lilly La More, the Vampire Vixen. She made other dogs lose their cool too. Some of them lost a lot, lot more. (Sometimes I think Rex nearly lost his sense of humour because of her!)

Rex says that the paranormal can always be explained.

He keeps telling me never to accept things at face value.

One quiet day in the office,
I was doing a bit of filing and Rex
was up to level three of
Pro Celebrity Sheepdog Trials©
on his Gameboy.
There was a knock on the door.

Flock!

Flock!

Flock!

Flock!

Flock!

Can you answer
the door, Franky? I've
just got to the tricky bit.
Does that door knocker
need oiling again?

I'm on
my way.

I opened the door to a whole flock of sheep!

It's a funny thing. There are two types of dog: the hunter and the protector. Well, something about those sheep really brought out the hunter in me. I felt like chasing them down the street and sinking my teeth into their little woolly bottoms!
I guess I'm not the sheepdog type.

They *were* clients. I had to keep myself under control.

We'd rather wait outside, thank you.

That made me feel like chasing them even more. They knew it too. They refused to come inside until they had seen Rex.

Rex came to the door to see
what all the fuss was about.
He gave them one of his looks.

They gave him a
sheepish look back
and became quiet.

Then they trotted into
the office like...
like little lambs.
Rex has such a masterful
way with some animals.

Jip had been the World Champion. Now he presented the Monday Night Sheepdog Trials. Jip was a star! The sheep gave us Jip's phone number. When Rex called him, Jip suggested we meet at the TV studio.

Rex was Jip's biggest fan. He must
have brushed himself at least three
times before we went!
Jip came out of his office to meet us.
I have to admit he was the most
handsome dog I'd ever seen.

I do understand. My grandfather was a sheepdog, so you could say that protecting sheep is in my blood.

Then why don't you come to the Ancient Society of Sheepdogs tomorrow? You could meet some of the other dogs with worried flocks.

I'll see you there. By the way, I don't suppose I could have your autograph? It's for my mother, you know.

Oh! How embarrassing.

The next day Rex went to the Shepherds' Hall.

Rex, old chap, how good to see you again.

Hello, Jip. My, this is an impressive place.

Jip introduced Rex to some of the members. A few of them were Champions in their own right.

If any of this got out, the newspapers would have a field day.

You can just see the headlines: **Aliens Ate My Flock!**

The TV ratings would drop. It would be the end of Monday Night Sheepdog Trials.

That would be terrible. I'll make this a top priority case.

We really had to see the
Hounds of Darkness for ourselves.
Jip's flock had told us that the
hounds usually appeared on
Saturday nights.
The next Saturday, we got ourselves
ready. We filled up our backpacks
with a thermos of coffee and
sandwiches

Better bring
your hanky,
Franky.

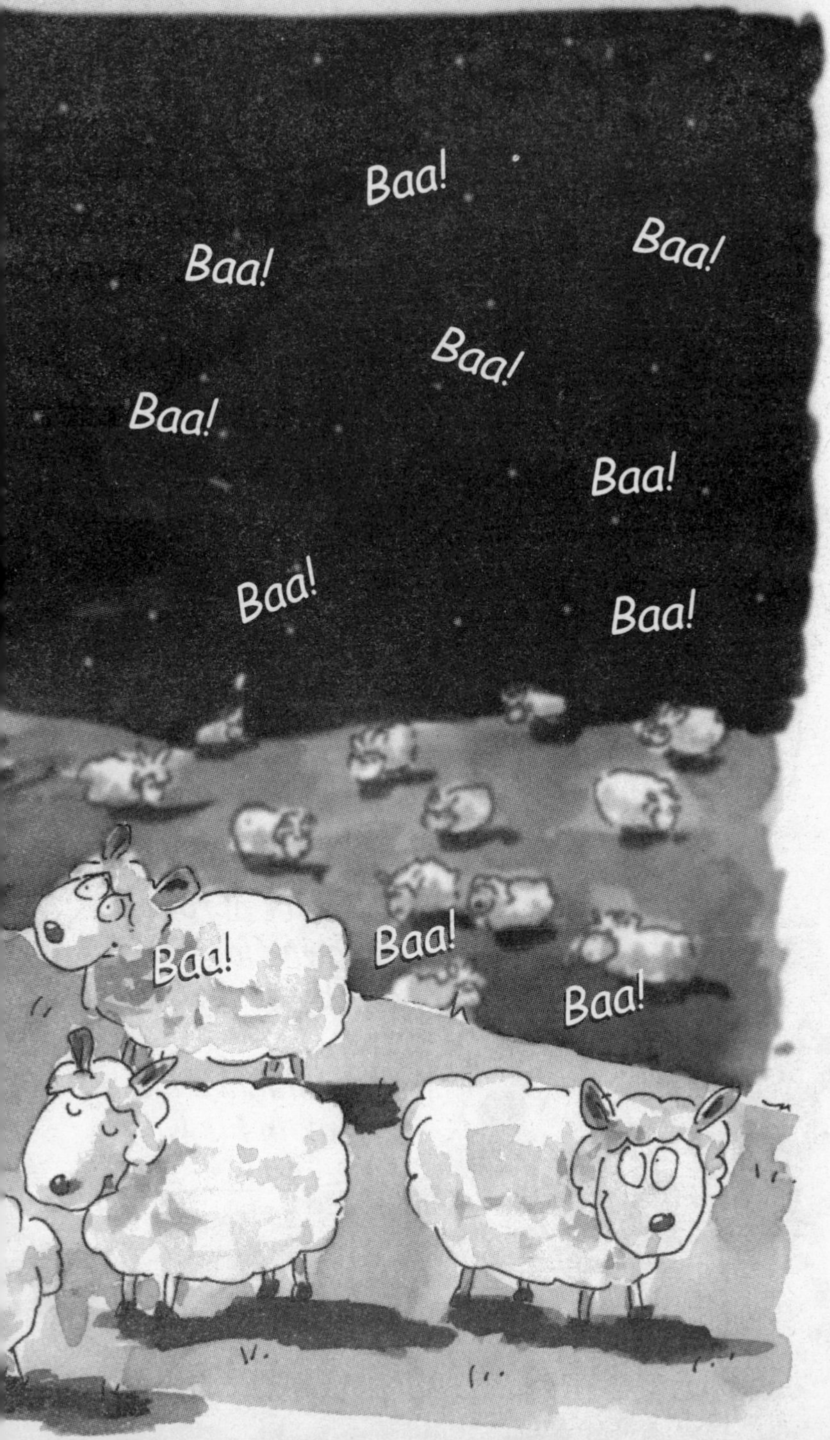
Baa!
Baa!
Baa!
Baa!
Baa!
Baa!
Baa!
Baa!
Baa!
Baa!
Baa!

Rex offered Shep one of our sandwiches and asked him some questions about the business of shepherding.

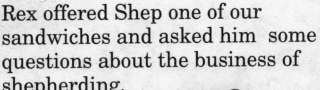

Do you do a lot of flock-sitting?

Yes. No one can look after a flock twenty-four hours a day, seven days a week. You need a break every now and then.

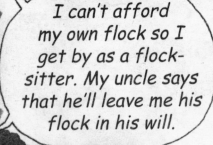

I can't afford my own flock so I get by as a flock-sitter. My uncle says that he'll leave me his flock in his will.

Call me biased, but I think sheep are the most stupid animals on the surface of the Earth. Rex always says that we need to understand the animals that we try to help. He says we should try to see the world through their eyes.
As far as I'm concerned all sheep are good for is eating grass and saying "Baa"!

The sheep were quite easy with Rex as he passed among them asking questions about the Hounds of Darkness.

If ever I went near a sheep I got this funny feeling.

The sheep edged away from me. Somehow, I couldn't make myself like them.

Do you know, I swear those sheep
carried on eating grass in their sleep!
And they sleep-bleat too.
All night long, baa, baa, baa!

We sat down with our coffee and
looked up at the stars. At quarter
past two the noises started. The
sheep became restless.

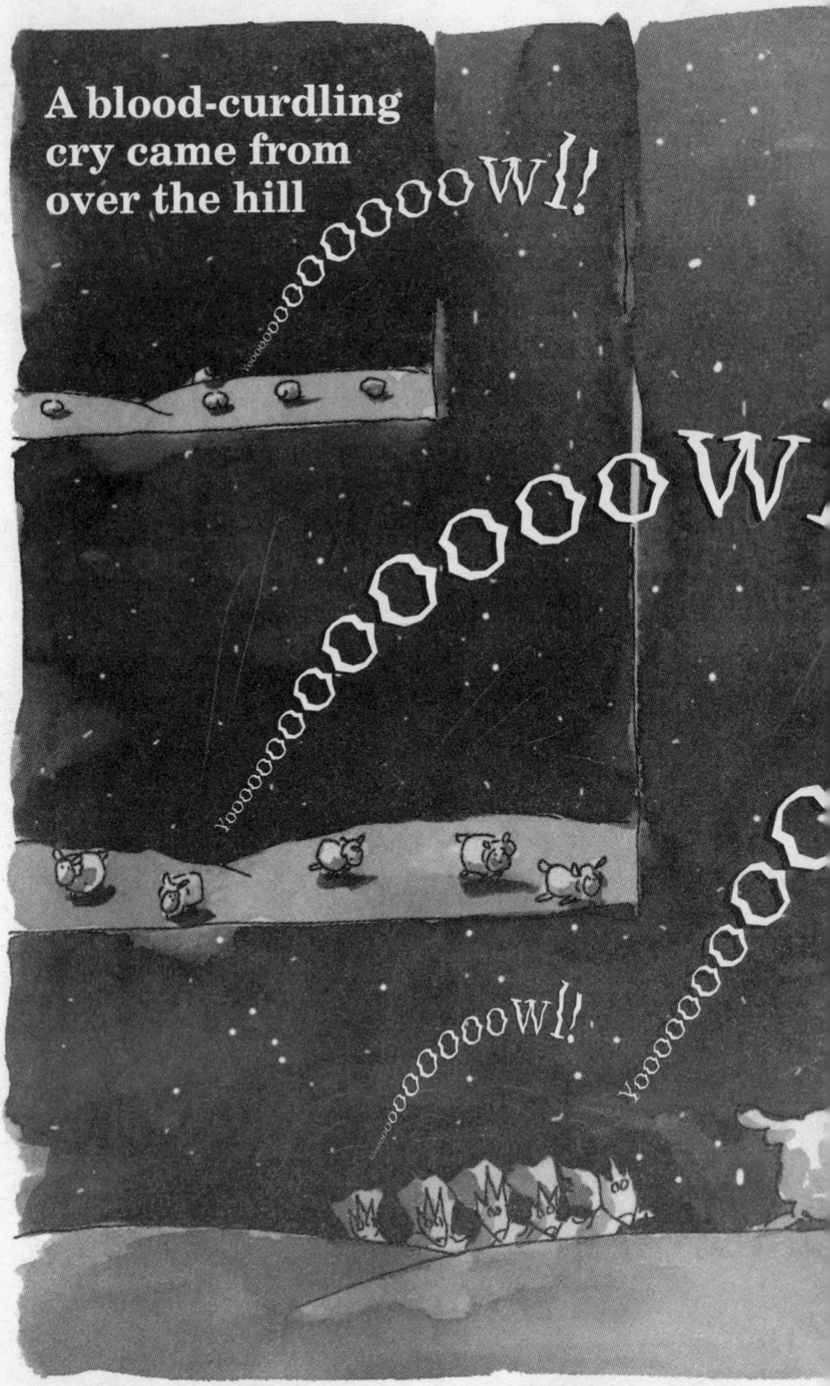
A blood-curdling cry came from over the hill

Strange, terrifying shapes raced
towards us!

The sheep panicked.
They ran as fast as they
could. Being sheep they all
stayed together in one flock.

Wearing strange flowing, glowing costumes, the Hounds of Darkness chased the sheep across the hillside, snapping at their heels and laughing crazily.

They were scary all right. Rex and Shep chased after them, but the hounds were way too fast for them.

Hiiaaah!
aaaaaaaaaaachOOOO!
It does look like fun, though!
Hiiaaah!

After a while the sheep collapsed with exhaustion and the hounds ran away. They were obviously only interested in the thrill of the chase. Poor Gracie was dead. She really had had a heart attack this time.

When Jip returned he was devastated.

We left them to their grief.

Rex spotted a small piece of white card lying on the grass. It glowed in the moonlight.

What is it?

It looks like a visiting card.

Congratulations!
You've been chased by
The Baa-Baa Club

9

A few days later, Jip phoned to let Rex know that he'd been elected as a member of the Ancient Society of Sheepdogs.

The Ancient Society of Sheepdogs was built to impress, and it did! While Rex sorted out the formalities of his new membership, I looked at the notice-board.

The main hall was full of sheepdogs.
I felt like I knew them all. They'd all
been on TV. Some of them were real
stars.

They certainly seemed to think highly of Rex.

10

Rex was all cheesy smiles. He was loving every minute of it. So was I. Hanging around with celebrities is what most of us dream about.

But as soon as we got out of the
building and were safely round the
corner, the smile dropped from Rex's
face.

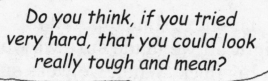

The next time Jip had a night off we made sure we were with his flock. When we were sure that Jip had gone, Rex told Shep and the sheep about his plan.

We practised Rex's plan.

Then we settled down to wait for the Hounds of Darkness.

Just after two in the morning…

The sheep very nearly panicked. I gave them such a growling, they didn't know who to fear most, me or the hounds. I felt rather powerful!

The hounds raced after the flock, shrieking with laughter.
They seemed to be having such fun, it was hard not to run off and join in. The sheep were doing their job. The hounds didn't know it, but they were being lured into a trap.

While the sheep went the long way, Rex and I took the short-cut to the old barn.

The flock ran straight for the barn.
Like a blurred woolly cloud they
rushed inside...

...and straight out of the back door.

As soon as they were through,
Rex slammed the back doors shut.

The hounds thought they had the
flock trapped in the barn. They
yelped with excitement and dived in.
As soon as the last one entered,
I heaved the heavy front doors shut.

We had them trapped inside!

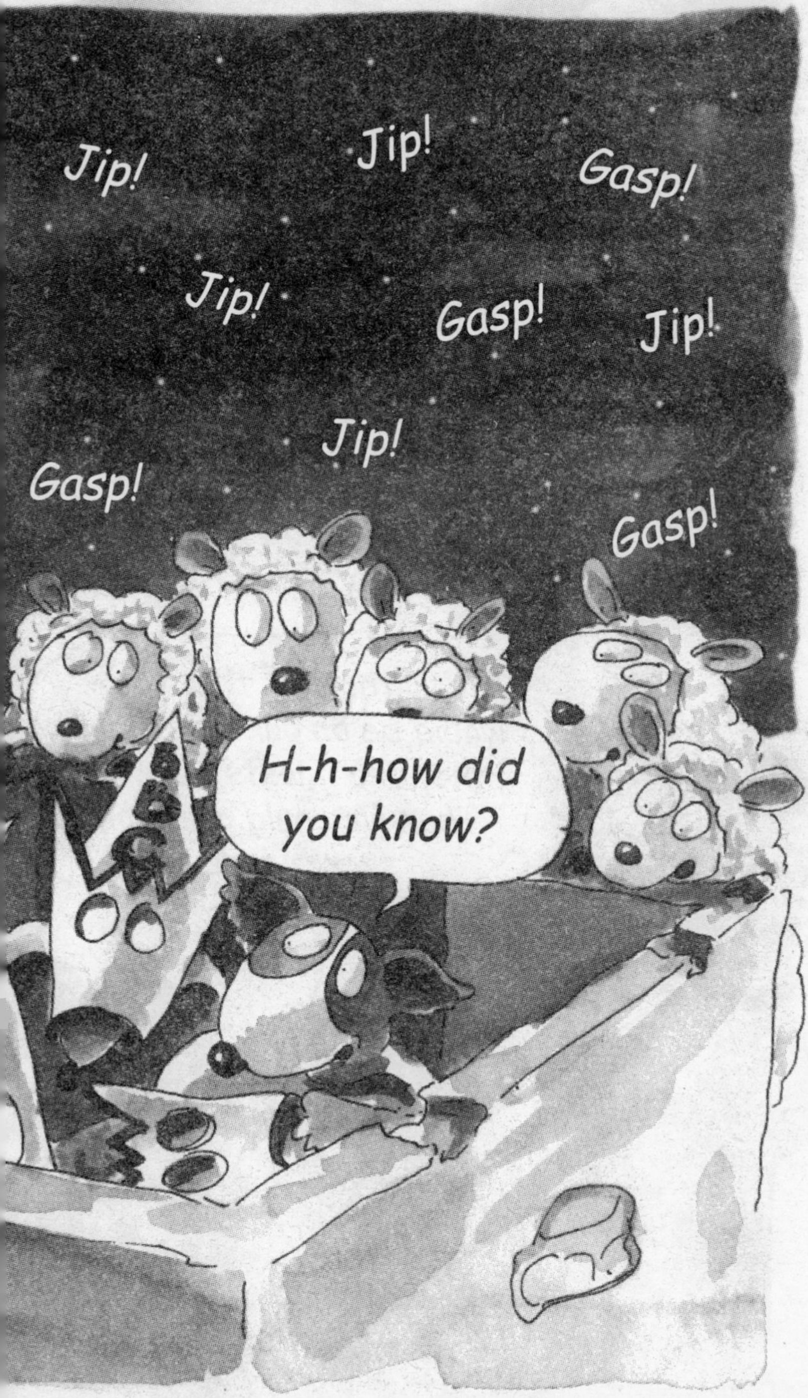
Jip!
Jip!
Gasp!
Jip!
Gasp!
Jip!
Jip!
Gasp!
Gasp!
H-h-how did you know?

13

Jip came to see us a few days later. He could hardly look us in the eye.

You can't imagine the pressure that TV sheepdogs are under. We have to be perfect all the time. We started the Baa-Baa Club as a little bit of fun. It just got a bit out of control.

I thought that you would be on our side and say that the ghosts were real. Then we could carry on in secret forever.

When Jip had gone, Rex told me how he'd worked it all out.

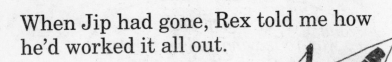

The hounds had the letters BBC embroidered on their costumes.

BBC
SAT
8th. June

When I saw their calling card, I remembered the cards on the Society notice-board.

They were secret signs for members of the Baa-Baa Club. They told the date of the next meeting, but meant nothing to the other honest dogs.

Order Form

THE REX FILES BOOKS ARE:

0 340 71432 8   The Life Snatcher
0 340 71466 2   The Phantom Bantam
0 340 71467 0   The Bermuda Triangle
0 340 71468 9   The Shredder
0 340 71469 7   The Frightened Forest
0 340 71470 0   The Baa-Baa Club

If you enjoyed this book you may want to read more about Rex and Franky,
or other books by Shoo Rayner, like *The Ginger Ninja*, a wonderful series of
books about a young cat called Ginger.

Ginger is a happy kitten.
He likes all his school friends,
loves playing pawball,
and even enjoys his lessons!
Until Tiddles comes to St Felix's . . .
When Tiddles joins the class,
it's soon clear he may be the
biggest bully the school
has ever known . . .

If you would like to read more about Ginger
(and find out how he becomes best friends with Tiddles),
the Ginger Ninja books are available at your local bookshop
or newsagent, or may be ordered direct from the publisher.

Phone 01235 400414 and have your credit card ready.

0 340 61955 4   The Ginger Ninja
0 340 61956 2   The Return of Tiddles
0 340 61957 0   The Dance of the Apple Dumplings
0 340 61958 9   St Felix for the Cup
0 340 69379 7   World Cup Winners
0 340 69380 0   Three's a Crowd

Please allow the following for postage and packing:
UK & BFPO – £1.00 for the first book, 50p for the second book, and 30p for
each additional book ordered up to a maximum charge of £3.00.

OVERSEAS & EIRE – £2.00 for the first book, £1.00 for the second book,
and 50p for each additional book.